The Lost Daughter and the Native Son.

By Kembabazi Emilly

Introduction:

The story is about Angela, a young lady whose life has much promise, whose dream is to help her parents and her local community build a better and brighter future. Sadly her 'worldly' success becomes a distraction, and she becomes consumed by selfish concerns. She forgets her dream, but her mother's unfailing trust and love eventually wins her daughter back. The daughter's journey towards self-transformation is energised by repentance. She recognises what she has failed to be - she is missing her life purpose - but all is not lost: she turns around and embraces the forgiveness of her mother.

It's also about other family members and the wider community of the village of Lama. Elijah, Angela's first husband, reminds us of Boaz from the book of Ruth in the Old Testament. He redeems lives through practical compassion and works of mercy. He even becomes a son to Samantha (Angela`s mother) and exemplifies that quality so strongly necessary in a community of love: self-sacrificing love - what the New Testament describes as *agape* love.

In fact, this is a poignant and very sad story; yet, thankfully, with a focus on redemption - there is hope because, at the very end, people's lives are transformed and transfigured. This note of joy takes a long time to come. The peace of forgiveness and reconciliation is won in spite of many obstacles.

If I could choose one word to pinpoint the essence of this story, this would be *COMPASSION*. I would therefore recommend this book to every person who seeks to know and understand the nature of compassion.

I will not 'spoil' your enjoyment by providing a detailed summary of the plot. Every person must read this book for themselves, with an inquiring mind and an open heart. This is a 'treasure-chest' of all of those values which make our human life, lived within society, valuable; more than that, without such values, loving relationships between human beings would be impossible.

In conclusion, it's all about dreams - worthwhile dreams. Those God-given dreams which, if acted upon, build a better world. Inspired by this story, we need to 'run with' our dreams - those dreams which God has placed at the innermost core of our beings, and rejoice in the transformation which this brings. We ourselves, and the world in which we live, will never be the same again.

The Lost Daughter and the Native Son.

Angela was a young girl who had been born in Lama Village; the only and much beloved daughter of Benjamin and Samantha. They nicknamed her Princess.

Angela`s parents were the poorest people in the whole village. Their house was grass thatched, and the walls were made using mud and cow dung.

Nevertheless, Angela continually promised her parents that she would build them a good permanent house when she grew up. They were always comforted by the hope which her words kindled in them: that one day they would be able to live a decent life.

Their neighbours had a lot of land and stores where they kept food, comprising dried harvests for sale and home consumption. Angela`s parents owned a very small piece of land, where they grew food crops only for home consumption.

They also had a traditional granary in their compound, which Benjamin had made himself.

Making a granary was cheap. All Benjamin needed was some grass for the roof and poles to support it. To make the walls and floor, he only needed mud and wattle. It was a round-shaped structure of about eight feet in circumference, raised at least 3 feet above the ground. The walls and floor were plastered with cow dung, to fill up the holes and smooth the finishing.

Their granary had a spherical and removable roof, similar to a kettle lid, which they could open and climb inside, either to store or remove the harvest. The stores included finger millet, beans, corn and cowpeas, to help in case of famine and also for future planting.

Although Benjamin and Samantha had not attended any school, they were so creative. They knew how to make pots out of clay, and taught this skill to Angela.

They would then carry the pots on their heads to the nearby market for sale. This was their only source of income.

In spite of their low level of income, they had a dream like any other parents: to give their daughter an education and to help her to go to University. They vowed to work hard to make their dream come true.

Angela was already in Primary Six. She had been a day student since kindergarten. Her wish and prayer was to join a boarding school after her primary education.

A year later, Angela was promoted to Primary Seven. She was determined to get the best grades to enable her to join a secondary school. Her parents had also promised her that she would join a boarding school, if she did well in her final examinations.

Throughout the year Angela performed well, and in her final exams she got a first grade.

Her parents were so proud of her, and very happy with her outstanding performance.

Angela`s dream came to pass when she was given a place at Mantha Secondary School. The school was somewhat expensive, but Angela`s parents wanted a school with excellent standards which would help their daughter to achieve the best academically.

It was time for Angela to report to her new school! Having never been to a boarding school before, she was very excited. Her parents had bought her a school uniform, shoes, and a few scholastic materials.

However, they had not yet bought her a mattress, bed sheets and a blanket; and they had been told that every student was required to report with at least half of the school fees. As they were still uncertain what to do, Benjamin got an idea.

He suggested that they give their one-inch mattress, a pair of bed sheets and a blanket to Angela, instead of buying new ones on the little money which they had saved for school fees. Samantha welcomed the idea.

It would have been so easy for them if Angela had her own mattress at home, but she did not have one. She had been sleeping on a mat since her childhood. So, her mother cleaned their mattress, blanket and bed sheets.

Angela could hardly hold back her tears, as she looked at her parents running up and down, doing what they could to ensure that she reported to school on time with the things that she needed

Angela said, "Dad, Mom, I promise you that I will never disappoint you. I will read hard, so that one day I make you proud.

"That's our prayer, Angela," Samantha and Benjamin said to their daughter.

At mid-day, Angela and her parents left for school. Although there were means of transport in her village,

Benjamin and Samantha wanted to use the little money they had frugally. So, they helped Angela to carry the mattress, her bag, basin and everything they had packed for her.

The school was about five kilometres from their home. They walked from home to school. By the time they reached the school, they were very tired, but extremely happy because their daughter was joining a boarding school.

On arrival, the school principal welcomed them and directed Benjamin to the Bursar's office. Benjamin was able to pay half of the school fees. Then the school matron took Angela and her parents to the dormitory, so Benjamin and Samantha could see where their daughter was going to reside.

The matron got Angela a bed and explained to her all the do's and don'ts of the boarding students.

This seemed unbelievable for Angela and her parents! This is because they were known as very poor people in Lama Village. Their neighbours thought Benjamin and Samantha would not be able to afford to pay for their daughter to go to secondary school, especially a boarding school.

At exactly 6 p.m., Angela was told by her dorm-mates that it was time to go to the dining room for dinner. She then accompanied her parents to the school gate and said goodbye to them.

Benjamin and Samantha left the school and went back home. Since they had given away their bedding to their daughter, they were going to sleep on the mat. They no longer had bed sheets or a blanket, but Samantha had a traditional long dress, which she cut in half to use as bed sheets.

The news of Angela having joined a good boarding school spread across Lama Village. Many of Samantha and Benjamin's village mates felt jealous of their prosperity. Instead of congratulating them, they laughed at them, saying, "Let us see whether Samantha and Benjamin will manage to pay her school fees! Of course, she will drop out. They cannot afford the fees."

However, a lady called Isabella, one of the local neighbours with a kinder heart, silenced them. She said, "With great determination, nothing is impossible. Although the school fees are expensive, there is no doubt Angela will study, even go to University, because she is a brilliant girl and her parents are very strong-minded." Turning towards Angela's parents, she said, "Benjamin and Samantha, congratulations on this achievement."

Deeply touched by the generosity of Isabella's spirit, Benjamin and Samantha replied, "Thank you, Isabella, for your kind words."

Isabella and her husband were close friends to Angela's parents. They were in their early seventies, but with no child after forty years of marriage. The couple loved Angela as if she was their own child. Angela helped them on many occasions by fetching water and fire wood.

Isabella and her husband were retired army soldiers. Having retired, they received a pension from the government every month. They pledged to support Angela with her education, by paying half of the school fees until she completed her studies at high school.

Samantha and Benjamin appreciated their generosity very deeply and gave thanks for them. It was a big relief! Even so, they continued to make pots and sell them until Angela completed her high school studies.

Every year the school arranged farewell parties for all of the candidate classes. Awards in different categories were given to the best students: those excelling in both discipline and academic studies.

In the year in which she completed high school, Angela was given awards in all of the categories: in both discipline and academic studies. She then went home for a vacation. During her vacation, Angela helped her parents with home chores and gardening.

One afternoon, Angela and her parents were busy in the garden. They heard Isabella calling Angela loudly. They became fearful. "What's the problem, Aunt Isabella?" Angela asked her.

"Is there any problem, Isabella?" Samantha added.

"This is unbelievable! But I knew it! I knew this would happen!" Isabella continued to shout.

"But Isabella, please tell us! You are scaring us. What's wrong?" Benjamin was anxious to know.

"Nothing is wrong, Benjamin. Everything is okay! I have good news for all of you!" Isabella exclaimed.

"News? About what, Isabella?" Benjamin enquired.

"About Angela! Our very own Angela! We have just heard her name on the radio. She has been given a full scholarship at Lam University to study Civil Engineering," Isabella explained.

"Hooooooo! Wooooooo! Yeeeeee!" Angela and her parents shouted uncontrollably, running around in the garden. It was indeed good news! It was talked about all over the village of Lama. No one in the whole village had ever been given a scholarship to the University. Angela had broken the record.

Isabella and her husband drove to the town immediately, and bought a big cake and drinks. They then invited Angela, her parents and a few people in the neighbourhood to a celebration. There was great jubilation!

In her speech, Angela attributed her success to her parents, Isabella and her husband, and the entire School of Mantha.

A few months later, Angela joined the University. As she had a scholarship, she stayed in one of the University dormitories. During all of her years of study, she never needed to re-take any exams. Her performance was excellent in all of her subjects. She had a great determination to study civil engineering, and she wanted to learn all about civil engineering to help her village develop strong infrastructure. She was awarded a first-class degree.

One can describe Angela as a fortunate, blessed and highly favoured person. This is because, after having gained her first degree, she was awarded another scholarship to study for a Masters Degree. She then continued her studies, and was awarded a PHD. She was no longer addressed as Angela but as Dr. Angela.

However, after acquiring her PHD, she obtained a very well-paying job in the city. She made a lot of investments, including companies, hotels and schools amongst other assets. She drove good cars. Sadly, from the time she had joined the University; she changed a lot and became a different person.

Angela never returned home. She forgot about her parents who had struggled to pay her school fees. She forgot the hardships they had gone through. She forgot all the promises she had made to her parents. It seemed that she no longer cared to know how they were doing. She forgot the village and her dreams of improving the village.

After some time, Angela met a handsome man, Elijah, who wanted to marry her. Elijah was a lawyer by profession who owned his own law firm. Angela dismissed his questions about her parents, saying, "Don't mind about them. My parents are just in the village."

Even though he begged her on many occasions to take him to see her parents, Angela refused. When Elijah persisted with his request, she told him that she did not have parents, and that she was the only child in the family. She proposed that they hold their engagement and wedding ceremonies in the city.

When her boyfriend heard about her sad story, he felt sorry and accepted her proposal. On the wedding day, no one from Angela`s family attended the ceremony. Her very own biological parents, and Isabella and her husband - who had supported her until she completed high school - did not receive invitations.

As Angela and Elijah were well-known in the city, their wedding ceremony was attended by a lot of people. It was even screened live on television.

In Lama Village, very few people owned a television set. However, Isabella and her husband had one. They liked watching news programmes.

One of the programmes they enjoyed the most was about parties and weddings. Having switched on the TV, they saw someone resembling Angela making marriage vows in the church. Initially they didn't think it was Angela, because she had left the village when she was seventeen years of age and very slim. The lady they now saw on TV was big and was addressed by others as Dr. Angela.

They continued to watch the programme, which they enjoyed; but when they looked at the lady getting married more carefully, they realised that she was the very same Angela whom they had known so many years previously. When the wedding ceremony was complete the couple proceeded to the reception. Isabella and her husband could not remain quiet any longer, as what they had seen astonished them.

"How could this happen?" they wondered to themselves.

"How could Angela do this to her parents? The parents who struggled and stood the laughter of this village, to ensure that she went to school? So, this is how she has paid them? Oh, she studied and got a PHD, and she now feels ashamed of her own parents?"

Isabella was speechless. She remembered how many of the villagers had laughed at Angela`s parents when Angela had just joined a boarding school; and the way in which Angela's parents had suffered every weekend, carrying pots on their heads up to the market. When Isabella recalled how they had given away their own bedding to her, she burst into tears.

Her husband left the house immediately to call Samantha and Benjamin. "Please come and see your daughter on the television," he said loudly.

"What? You mean, Angela?" they asked.

"Yes," he replied.

"No! Not our Angela!" they shouted at Isabella's husband.

As soon as they reached Isabella's home, they heard Angela's husband giving a speech on the TV. They sat down and listened carefully.

Angela's husband said, "Thank you all for coming. My wife, Angela, and I are very happy today. I think I am one of the luckiest men in the world, because the beautiful lady you can see beside me is highly educated. She holds a PHD. She is called Dr. Angela: a renowned engineer and investor."

"But you can't imagine." He paused as he was on the verge of tears. Having regained composure he then resumed his speech. "I am sorry for being so emotional, but it's so sad that Dr. Angela's parents are not here with us.

If they were still alive, they would be so happy to see their daughter getting married."

He continued, "Personally I never got a chance to know her parents. When Angela and I met, I really wanted to know her home and her precious parents. In fact, I had planned to hold our engagement ceremony at their home, and then the wedding here in the city; but she told me that she doesn't have parents, and that she is the only child in her family. It's so sad! May their souls rest in eternal peace."

Elijah felt so sad and tearful that he could not hold the microphone any longer. He just handed it over to his wife, Angela, so she could say a word. She said, "To you, my dear husband, I love you so much; and it's a pity that my parents are not here with us. They went to be with the Lord. But, it's okay, darling, life has to continue."

Everyone in the audience felt sorry for Angela; especially her husband, Elijah. Angela was a shameless daughter!

Her dad had a heart attack and collapsed after hearing the speech. Isabella and her husband helped to rush him to the hospital. Benjamin received treatment but, very sadly, he didn't make it and died a few weeks later.

The news of Benjamin's death left the people of Lama feeling very sad, even though they didn't know the cause of his death. During the funeral service, Samantha narrated the whole story to the mourners.

"What?" Everyone was astonished.

"How could Angela do such a thing to her parents?" they wondered.

Angela did not know that her father had died and so did not attend his funeral.

As the years went by, Angela and her husband became more and more successful. However, although they had been married for fifteen years, Angela had not borne a child for her husband. She would cry day and night, wishing desperately to become pregnant, but it was all in vain.

Despite Angela's inability to conceive, her husband continued to love her very much. "Whether you have children or not, I will still love you, Angela," Elijah reminded her day after day.

Meanwhile Angela's mother was not in good health. She was getting old, and always worried about her house, which was deteriorating, with several cracks in the walls and a leaking roof.

Her neighbours Isabella and her husband would often ask her to move into their house for safety, but she always turned down their offer. Angela's mother still hoped that her daughter would come back for her one day.

Despite everything that Angela had done, Samantha still loved her with the heart of a mother.

One day, Angela`s husband decided to look for his childhood friend, Arnold, with whom he had studied from kindergarten up to primary seven. It had been thirty-seven years since they last seen or heard from each other.

Well, things can truly happen unexpectedly! Elijah, who expected to find his friend in a town called Laco, eventually met him in Lama Village where Angela had been born. How did this happen?

When Elijah arrived in Laco town he could not find his friend`s home. Thankfully he knew the first names of Arnold's father and mother. So, he immediately went to the house of the chairman of the local council.

Elijah told the chairman about the people he was looking for. Fortunately, the chairman knew them well. "I am sorry, sir. Arnold and his parents no longer live in this town," he said.

"Oh no! Where did they go, chairman?" Elijah asked.

The chairman replied, "You see, when Arnold completed his studies in Agriculture, it was not easy for him to get a job. His parents were still living in a rented house here in Laco, yet they had over three acres of land in Lama Village.

So, Arnold got the idea of farming. He went to the village and started growing all kinds of vegetables and food crops. Eventually, he started to earn a lot of money. He is now the one who supplies all of the food to the markets in this area.

He later built a good house for himself and his parents. They are now residents of Lama Village. Arnold is happily married with eight children."

"Wow! That is amazing," Elijah exclaimed.

Elijah was very happy about his friend's success. "Chairman, would you mind taking me to Arnold's home?" Elijah asked politely.

"It's okay, sir," the chairman replied.

He quickly jumped into Elijah`s car, who then drove to Lama village. It took about two hours to reach the village. Arnold and his family members had gone to the garden to harvest sorghum and so, were not at home.

The chairman did not wait for them to return home, as he knew where the garden was. "Please sir," he said to Elijah, "Stay here and I will go to the garden and call Arnold for you."

"Alright, thanks chairman," Elijah replied.

The chairman then rushed to the garden, where he found Arnold working. "Hello, Arnold, greetings to you and your family."

Arnold: "Greetings to you, too, Chairman. Is everything okay?"

Chairman: "Yes, all is well, thank you."

Arnold: "That's good to hear."

Chairman: "I have good news for you."

Arnold: "Good news for me? It's about what?"

Chairman: "It's about Elijah."

Arnold: "Elijah? Who is he?"

Chairman: "Your childhood friend!"

Arnold: "What? Where is he? Where did you see him?"

Chairman: "He came to Laco town looking for you"

Arnold: "Oh, my goodness! Why didn't you bring him here?"

Chairman: "Arnold, relax! I have come along with him. He is already at home waiting for you."

Arnold: "Unbelievable!"

Indeed, Arnold found it so hard to believe. The last time he saw Elijah was when they were still in primary school at the ages of eleven and twelve. Elijah was now forty-nine and Arnold forty-eight years old.

Accompanied by his family, Arnold rushed home to meet Elijah. Elijah recognised Arnold as soon as he saw him. He quickly ran and hugged him. He also greeted Arnold's family members.

Arnold: "Nice to see you, Elijah, after so many years!"

Elijah: "The pleasure is mine, Arnold."

Arnold: "You are most welcome in my home. Please, let's go inside and take a seat."

Elijah: "Thank you."

Arnold: "So where are you now? Where do you work? Are you married?"

Elijah: "Arnold, I am a lawyer by profession. I am self-employed. I own a law firm in Quanta city. Oh, yes! I am happily married to a beautiful wife, Dr. Angela."

Arnold: "Wow! I am so happy for you, Elijah."

Elijah: "Thank you, buddy."

Arnold: "So how did you meet your wonderful wife?"

Elijah: "I met her at one of the malls in the city when she was doing her shopping. We exchanged our phone numbers and became good friends.

Eventually we fell in love and I asked her to marry me after we had been going out with each other for four years."

Arnold: "That's wonderful!"

Elijah: "But, but"

Arnold: "But what, Elijah?"

Elijah: "Honestly, on our wedding day I really felt so sorry for her. I couldn't imagine how she was feeling."

Arnold: "What happened?"

Elijah: "None of her family members attended our wedding. Angela is the only child in her family, and her parents passed away when she had just joined high school. That's what she told me."

Arnold: "Oh, no! I am sorry to hear that. Have you ever visited her home?"

Elijah: "Unfortunately, no. I had wanted to hold our engagement ceremony at their home, but when I told her, she said that there was no need."

Arnold: "Doesn't she even have any relatives?"

Elijah: "No."

Arnold: "That's strange."

Elijah: "Why?"

Arnold: "Well, there is a similar family in this village"

Elijah: "Really?"

Arnold: "Yes! The girl was also called Angela. She was born into a very humble family. We actually studied together from secondary to high school. But what she did to her parents, it's unbelievable!"

Elijah: "What did she do?"

Arnold: "She disappointed them."

Elijah: "How?"

Arnold: "Well, her parents did all they could to ensure she was able to go to school. Thankfully, she performed well - excellent at all levels. She was given a full scholarship to study Civil Engineering at Lam University, the best University in this country."

Elijah: "What?"

Arnold: "Yes! From the day she joined the university, she changed completely. Angela has never returned home. She did not even invite her parents to her graduation ceremony. As if that was not enough, she held a big wedding ceremony in the city, but she did not invite any of her family members; not even her biological parents."

Elijah: "What? That's impossible! How could she do that?"

Arnold: "Their wedding ceremony was screened live on TV. During her speech, Angela said confidently that she did not have parents; that they had passed away, and that she did not have any family members or relatives."

Elijah: "Oh my goodness! How did her parents feel? Did they hear her speech?"

Arnold: "Yes, both her parents were watching the ceremony on TV. Her father had a heart attack, from which he sadly died. Her mother is now old and very weak. When you reach her home, and see the house she lives in, you will shed tears."

Elijah: "Oh dear."

As Elijah listened to this sad story, he was unable to hold back his tears. He was unable to believe that the Angela, whom Arnold was talking about, was his wife. Arnold did not know that Angela was Elijah`s wife or that she held a PHD.

After some time, Elijah asked Arnold whether he had the pictures of the Angela he had spoken about. "You said that you studied with Angela from secondary level to high school. Do you have any photos of her?"

"I do," Arnold replied. "In fact, I have many of them. The ones which we took as a group on the occasion of our high school farewell party, and also a photo of when Angela was giving a speech, after receiving awards for being the best student of the year in both academic studies and discipline."

Elijah began to suspect that the Angela of whom Arnold was speaking was the same person as Angela, his wife. He remembered that his wife had refused to take him to see her parents, before she had even explained to him that her parents had died.

"May I have a look?" Elijah asked to see the photos.

"Oh, sure, here are the photos," Arnold replied.

"Impossible! Arnold, this is impossible!" Elijah could not believe what he saw.

"Why?" Arnold asked.

"How? How can this be possible? Why did this happen to me?" Elijah looked very confused.

"What's wrong, Elijah? Is everything okay?" Arnold wondered what was happening.

"How can everything be okay, Arnold? I really don't know what to do now!" Elijah was crying. He was very upset. Looking at the photos over and over again, he exclaimed, "Angela, me and you, it's over!"

"What are you talking about, Elijah?" Arnold insisted.

"Arnold, she is my wife." Elijah said in a low and subdued tone.

"Who?" Arnold asked quickly.

"The Angela in the picture is my wife," he confirmed.

"What? Elijah, are you really sure of what you are saying?"

"Yes. But why did Angela lie to me? How could she do that to her parents who struggled for her? How could she be ashamed of her own parents? " Elijah was both upset and angry.

Arnold was shocked. He felt very sorry for Elijah. "How many children do you have now?"

"We have been married for fifteen years. However, we do not have any children. But that has not bothered me at all, because I loved Angela unconditionally. I feel so disappointed. Angela has broken my heart, Arnold!"

"I am sorry, Elijah. I can't even imagine how you feel right now."

"Arnold, would you mind taking me to Angela`s home?" he asked politely.

"Of course I don't, Elijah. Her home is not far from here," he said.

They got into the car and headed to Angela`s home. During the journey, Elijah's phone began to ring. The call was from his wife, Angela. Although Elijah was already upset with her, he decided to handle the conversation in a mature way. He picked up his phone.

"Hello, my love, did you reach well?" Angela asked.

Elijah: "Yes, I did. Thank you for asking."

Angela: "Were you able to find your friend"?

Elijah: "Yes, I did."

Angela: "Oh that's great. I expect you will have interesting stories to tell when you come back."

Elijah: "Yes. I do have something to tell you, but we won't talk about it now."

Angela: "Alright, my love. I can`t wait! When are you coming home?"

Elijah: "I'm not yet sure, but I will keep in touch."

Angela: "Okay then my love. But as you have found your childhood friend then you should be sounding so happy, but it sounds as if you are unhappy. Are you okay?"

Elijah: "I am fine. Don't worry."

Angela: "Okay, bye my love."

Elijah: "Bye."

Arnold and Elijah finally arrived at Angela`s home. Elijah could not control himself as he looked at Samantha's house. He burst into tears.

Samantha was inside the house sleeping as she was not in good health. But it was also threatening to rain outside. Arnold quickly knocked on the door. He kept on knocking, but Samantha did not come out. "I hope she is safe," Elijah said.

"Hello, hello, hello, Mrs. Samantha. It's Arnold." He thought that mentioning his name would help. Indeed, Samantha heard him knocking and calling her, but she was struggling to stand up and open the door. Also, she could not raise the volume of her voice sufficiently for Arnold to hear her.

After a few minutes, Samantha managed to open the door. Holding onto her walking stick, she came out. For the very first time in her life, she saw an expensive car parked in her compound.

"Whose car is this? Is it for my daughter, Angela?" she wondered.

Arnold swiftly greeted her, "Good afternoon, Mrs. Samantha?"

"Good afternoon, Arnold. You are welcome. I am just wondering who the owner of that car is? Now I know. It's yours," Samantha said.

"No. The car isn't mine. It belongs to the visitor who I have brought to see you," Arnold clarified.

"A visitor?" Samantha asked with a smile. She had a feeling that her daughter, Angela, had come to see her after so many years.

"You mean Angela has come?" Samantha asked.

"No. It's not Angela," Arnold confirmed to her.

This news made Samantha look very sad. She kept on wondering who the visitor might be. While Elijah was still moving around Samantha`s compound, he saw a young boy from the neighbourhood playing near Samantha's house.

"Hey, what's your name?" he asked.

"My name is Derrick," he replied.

"Sir, are you looking for Madam Samantha?" Derrick asked.

"Yes. Is she okay?" Elijah enquired.

"No," Derrick replied. "You see, Mrs. Samantha has a lot of problems. She doesn't even have a toilet. Imagine what that is like for someone of her age. She has a traditional pit latrine which fell apart many years ago. Every time she wants to go to the toilet, she has to visit her neighbours.

One night she was bitten by a cobra snake when returning home. Luckily enough, her closest friend, Mrs. Isabella took her for treatment immediately. Otherwise, she would have died.

"As you can see, she also doesn't have a kitchen. She has to cook outside on the veranda using firewood. When you enter her house, and see where she sleeps, and how the roof leaks, you truly feel sorry for her!"

The more Derrick talked about the challenges that Samantha was facing, the more Elijah felt upset with Angela.

"What kind of a woman did I marry?" Elijah wondered.

"Angela is a shameless woman. She is so deadly!" he concluded.

"Oh, there he comes," Arnold said.

"Who?" Samantha asked.

"Your visitor. He is called Elijah."

"Yes, that's right. My name is Elijah. I'm Arnold's childhood friend."

"Thank you for coming, Elijah." Samantha said.

"It's my pleasure, ma`am," he replied.

"Please, both of you, come inside the house and take a seat," Samantha suggested.

"Oh, sure," Elijah and Arnold said together.

Samantha had no chairs in her house. She only had two traditional wooden stools, which she gave them to sit on. The house had one bedroom with no door or curtain. Elijah and Arnold could easily see what was in her bedroom.

She had neither a bed nor a mattress. The only mattress on which she and her late husband had slept was given to Angela when she first started her studies at the boarding school.

Angela had even taken the same mattress with her to the University. She did not bring it back to her parents. Since that time, Samantha had been sleeping on an old mat.

"So, Elijah how was the journey?" she asked.

"It was okay, mother." He replied.

"How have you been, mother?" Elijah asked.

"It's a long story, my son," Samantha said. She told Elijah of how their own daughter had pronounced herself and Angela's father dead on her wedding day, and of how her husband had died of a heart attack due to what Angela had said.

"We last saw Angela when she was joining the University. Since then, she has never cared enough to come back to see us. She even doesn't know that her father passed away. Well, as she said in public, that she is an orphan, soon she will be a double orphan."

"Please don't say that, mother," Elijah said.

It's really true, my son. I have very few days left to live, because my health is deteriorating day by day. I rarely have anything to eat, as I no longer have the strength to dig in the garden. I also don't have medicines for my high blood pressure."

It upset Elijah to see Samantha weeping uncontrollably. Quickly hugging her, he said, "Things will be alright. Don't worry, mother." He then pulled out a hankie from his pocket and wiped her tears.

"It's okay, my son. You know what I have gone through is a lot, so at times it's very hard for me to control my emotions. Thanks for your words of encouragement. I now feel much relieved."

Samantha did not realise that she was talking to her son in-law. Elijah had decided not to introduce himself to her. He thought it was not yet the right time. He also cautioned Arnold not to tell anyone.

As they were still talking, it started to rain heavily. The house was leaking water everywhere. Elijah and Arnold saw how Samantha was struggling to fold her mat, and the rugs she used to cover herself, so as not to become wet.

"My goodness! This is so unfair. Really, she doesn't deserve to be in this situation," Samantha heard Elijah whispering into Arnold's ear.

"My sons, I am now used to living in this way. You don't need to worry about me. I have been in this situation for many years," she said. Samantha's expression was of someone who felt resigned to her circumstances.

Elijah suddenly had an idea. He proposed that all of them should get into his car for shelter. Arnold welcomed this idea, but Samantha seemed not to be happy with it. She said, "Please go. I will be okay. After all, it will not be long before the rain stops."

"No! We cannot leave you behind. Let's go," Elijah insisted. Quickly holding onto Samantha's hand, they both got into the car. Guess what happened next? Within minutes heavy winds came and the ensuing floods washed away Samantha's house.

"Oh, no! Oh no!" Everyone was shocked. Samantha was shaking with fear. Looking at Elijah, she said, "Elijah, who really sent you here?"

"No one, mother. I just came to visit Arnold, and when he told me about you, we decided that we would come and see you," he replied.

"This is unbelievable! I mean, if you hadn't come, I would be dead by now. You must be an angel!" Turning to Arnold, she said, "Thank you as well. If it wasn't for your friendship with Elijah, you both wouldn't have come."

Samantha, Elijah and Arnold had escaped narrowly! The news about what had happened went viral in the village community. In a few minutes almost all of the village residents had gathered at Samantha`s compound to witness what had happened. They thought that Samantha was no more.

Samantha, Elijah and Arnold were still inside the car, and could not be seen, as the windows were tinted. They got out of the car. "Samantha! Samantha!" the villagers shouted. They felt happy when they saw her. Isabella, her best friend, came quickly and hugged her. "How did you escape?" she asked.

"It's Elijah who made it possible. Elijah is a childhood friend of Arnold. They had come to see me. So, when it started to rain heavily, Elijah suggested that we should all get into his car for shelter.

And, as soon as we got into the car, the house fell down," Samantha explained, with tears rolling down her face."

Everyone was shocked. Indeed, it was a big shock! Because even though many residents had lost their crops and animals during the incident, but none of their houses were destroyed except that of Samantha. They felt sorry for her, but again thanked Elijah and his friend for rescuing her.

"Samantha, so what next? Are you coming with me to my house?" Isabella asked.

Elijah did not wait for Samantha to respond. He said to Isabella, "We are taking her. She will stay with us for the time being. In a few months, we will make sure that a new house is built for her here."

"Wow! Wow! There is a time for everything. It's time for Samantha to rise and shine!" one of the residents commented.

Elijah drove Samantha to Arnold's home. The family welcomed Samantha and made her feel at home. Immediately afterwards, accompanied by Arnold, Elijah drove into town and bought new clothes and jewellery for Samantha.

Elijah decided not to go to the city until Samantha's house was complete. He contacted some of his engineer friends who were living in a different city. They came and helped him to make a house plan.

The building work then began. Angela was not aware of what was going on at home. Elijah did not tell her what had happened to her mother's house and how they had all narrowly escaped death.

When Angela called, asking when he was going to come home, he told her this would be in a few months' time. "There is a project which Arnold and I are working on, but I hope it should be complete in four months, perhaps less."

"Alright, my love," Angela said.

"When the project is over, I will invite you," said Elijah.

"Okay," Angela agreed. "I would be happy, my love. What a brilliant idea!"

In three months' time, Samantha`s house had been completed and fully furnished. No-one in the village of Lama, or in the nearby towns, had such a house. The design of the house and the fence was unique.

Outside the main gate they put up a big sign post showing Samantha`s address: Samantha House, Block 219, Lama Village. During the three months Samantha had been staying at Arnold's home, she did not know how the building work was progressing until the end.

When everything had been done, Elijah arranged a home coming party for her.

Together with Arnold, he invited all the residents of Lama Village and some of his closest friends from the city.

The residents were pleased to accept his invitation and pledged to work hand in hand with him to ensure that the party went well.

Why did they pledge their support to someone they had only known for three months? Because the entire village of Lama had not had electricity before, although it was something they had wanted for a very long time. Some of them did not know what procedures would need to be followed; while others knew it would be costly. But Elijah, working together with the authorities, had done everything required, paying for the installation of electricity from his own finances.

Samantha's house, and all the houses in the village of Lama, had now been connected to the electricity supply! Everyone was overwhelmed by Elijah's kindness. He became their super-hero!

Did Elijah invite Angela to the party? Yes, he did. However, he did not tell her that the party would be in Lama. If he had done so, Angela would probably not have accepted the invitation. He asked one of his friends, Smith, to pick her up.

At first, Angela refused a lift, because she had her own car, which was an expensive model. Later on, however, she accepted. During the journey, Smith did not mention anything to her about the venue. Thankfully Elijah had sent him the address.

Smith's car had tinted windows so Angela could not look outside so easily. However, it had been over twenty years since she last visited home. The village had changed quite a lot. One area which had been open land was now occupied by farm buildings. So it was difficult for her to remember where she was heading to.

Elijah had arranged everything very well. There was plenty of food and drinks.

The residents contributed most of the items, which included food, fruits and traditional local brews.

The residents also came early in the morning to help with cooking, cleaning and organising. By mid-day everything was set, food and drinks were ready to be served, and slow music was playing in the background.

Everyone was waiting for the guest honour, who was none other than Samantha. Elijah and Arnold left to bring her. As the car approached the gate, she saw a big sign post with her name and address written on.

She looked at it clearly and asked, "What's all this, Elijah?"

Elijah stopped the car and opened the car door for her. As she was getting out, she saw lots of people sitting in beautifully decorated tents, which included her village mates and many other people she did not recognise.

"What a surprise!" She said.

It was indeed a surprise, as she did not know that everyone who lived in the village had been invited. They all stood up and clapped hands for her. They shouted, "Welcome back, Samantha. Congratulations!"

"But is this Samantha or someone else? Some residents were whispering to others. Samantha looked much younger and healthier, as she had been eating and sleeping well.

She looked so very different - the same Samantha, with the same qualities of character, only transformed; her beauty shone forth more clearly. Elijah had bought her expensive shoes, a very beautiful glittering dress, and a gold necklace and earrings. Her hair had been coiffed in a modern style, but one which was both modest and attractive.

She was the same person in the eyes of the residents, and yet somehow also different - a more vibrant and happy Samantha. She was seventy -two years old, but she looked much younger, due to the good care she had received when staying at Arnold's home.

While waving at the residents, she turned around and saw the house which Elijah had built for her. "Oh, my goodness! What's this?" Samantha shouted. She did not care that she was now old, and that she was wearing very smart clothes; she jumped over and over again just like a teenager. As she was about to kneel down to thank Elijah, he interrupted her. "No! No! Please don't do that. You are like a mother to me. I respect you so much."

"Unbelievable! But who exactly are you, Elijah? I mean your kindness and support to me is beyond what I thought possible, and I cannot repay you." There were tears in Samantha's eyes as she said this.

"You deserve more than this, mother," said Elijah. "Wipe away your tears and smile, because a new chapter of your life has just begun. Many more good things are yet to come your way, mother. Here are the keys for your house."

Elijah, Arnold and a few people from the audience then led Samantha to the house. Amidst applause from the audience, she cut the ribbon that was tied to the balcony.
She then opened the house. "Wow! This is so beautiful, Elijah!" she said.

"I am glad you like it, mother," Elijah said with a big smile.

Samantha then walked into the sitting room. She was surprised to see many of her family photos. Elijah had re-developed and framed every photo in the album.

These included photos of when Samantha and Benjamin were teenagers and of their wedding; and of Angela at different times of her life: when she was a baby, a teenager and of her high school graduation.

The photo that touched Samantha the most was the one of Benjamin, Angela and herself carrying pots heading to the market. Having cried for some time, she then burst into laughter. "Where did you get all these, Elijah?" she asked.

"From your best friend, Mrs. Isabella," he replied.

"I see! You know when my other house developed big cracks; I took my photo album to her for safety. What a brilliant idea! Thank you so much for this, Elijah," Samantha was very happy. "You are welcome, mother," Elijah replied.

Samantha was delighted by her new sitting-room. There was a big television and a sofa: things which Samantha had longed for since she was a child.

"Oh! I now know that it really doesn't matter how many years it takes before your dream comes true. What matters is your positivity towards your dream," she confessed.

When she entered the master bedroom, she was speechless. She had never seen such a beautiful bed before. She was so excited! She quickly jumped onto it and took a rest. Then she fell asleep and started to snore loudly. Everyone burst into laughter.

"Hey mother? Mother? Mother? Please wake up!" Elijah called to her.

"Oh sorry, I felt so peaceful, I went to sleep," she apologised.

Arnold and Elijah then led her to her seat. Food was served as well as drinks.

Sometime later, Samantha cut her cake and the ushers helped her to serve it to the residents.

Samantha was then called upon to say a word. She said, "even though my own daughter abandoned me and considered me dead, it became a blessing in disguise!" Samantha laughed. "I mean, I have got a son, Elijah, who has done all this for me. Honestly, words cannot express how happy and thankful I am."

As she was still speaking, the car in which her daughter was travelling arrived at the gate. Angela saw the sign post. She asked, "Where are we now, Mr. Smith?"

"At last, we have arrived, Angela! We are in a village called Lama," he replied.

"Lama? What a coincidence? I also come from Lama, but this place looks so different from my home village." Angela looked nervous and confused because her mother`s name was written on the sign post.

"Mr. Smith, are you sure we are in the right place?" Angela picked up her phone immediately and called Elijah. "Hello, love. I think we are lost. Where did you tell him to bring me?"

"Okay, where are you?" Elijah asked.

"Well, where we are, there is a big sign post which reads Samantha House, Block 219, Lama Village. Are we far from where the party is?" Angela asked.

"No! You are in the right place. The gate is open. Let the car enter," Elijah said.

Having arrived at the house, Angela could not believe her eyes. She recognised her mother and almost everyone else. As soon as the residents recognised Angela, their faces changed. Led by Isabella and her husband, they quickly surrounded the car and started to confront her. "Have you forgotten what you did to your parents, Angela? Are you not ashamed of coming here?

You are a disgrace not only to your parents, but also to the entire village of Lama!"

Angela almost fainted. "Enough of this!" Samantha shouted loudly. She couldn't withstand what was going on. She approached the car and asked everyone to keep quiet. With tears rolling from her eyes, she said, "irrespective of what Angela did, she is still my daughter. My only child! She was lost, and was found."

Having heard what her mother said, Angela got the courage to get out of the car. She embraced her mother. "You have never changed, mother. Your love and compassion is still the same. You are my hero!" Angela said in a voice trembling with emotion.

She quickly got down onto her knees and apologised to her mother. "I am sorry, mother, for all of the pain I caused you and dad. I went astray and never fulfilled what I had promised to both of you. Please forgive me. Please mother?"

Samantha was calm. "It's okay, Angela. I have been waiting for this day for over twenty years!"

Angela looked puzzled. "You have been waiting for this day? What about dad? Where is he?" Angela thought that both of her parents were still alive. "Mother, where is dad?"

Samantha was silent for a moment before replying, "He passed away, Angela."

Angela: "What? When? How?"

Samantha: "Yes! Angela. It's now been fifteen years since your dad passed away."

Angela: "Oh no! Was he sick? What was the cause of his death?"

Samantha: "Angela, it's a long and sad story. We better not talk about it."

Angela: "No, mother. Please, tell me. What was he suffering from?"

Samantha: "Well, your dad and I saw your wedding on the television."

Angela: "No! No! Is that true, Mother?"

Samantha: "Yes! We even heard the speech you made, when you said that your parents had passed away, and that you did not have any family members left. We were so shocked. Angela, your dad died of a heart attack."

Angela: "Dad! Dad! What happened to your daughter, Angela? Your only daughter who you loved most! How could I do such a thing to you, dad! Please forgive me for the pain and shame that I brought to this family!" Angela cried loudly.

She felt very ashamed and guilty. She was also wondering how Elijah had found her home, and how she was going to rectify the lies she had told him: that she was a double orphan and had no relatives.

Speaking into the microphone, Elijah said, "Angela, so now you know all the pain and shame that you have brought to this family? Because of you, your dad passed away. Do you even know that recently your mother also narrowly escaped death? If Arnold and I had not come to her house, she would be no more."

"Angela, you sleep in a well furnished mansion. You own commercial houses and five star hotels in the city. You eat what you want, you dress expensively, you drive expensive cars, and above all, you are a well-known engineer. I was shocked when I found your mother in a ram-shackle grass-thatched house, and sleeping on rags. Imagine! Your own mother had no food to eat, and she did not have even a toilet or bathroom.

While there, it rained. She invited us into the house. Oh my goodness! She had no chair but only two traditional wooden stools.

The house had big cracks that you could easily see outside. The roof was leaking very badly. We spoke with her for some time, but later I suggested that we all go to my car for shelter. We had only just got into the car when the house collapsed. That's how we all survived, Angela."

Elijah continued. "Angela, who can be better than your mother, who carried you for nine months in her womb? And your late dad who sacrificed everything he had to ensure that you went to the best schools. Believe me, Angela, you would not be who you are now, if your parents had not sacrificed all they had for you!

Having seen the situation in which your mother was living, I decided to build her a better house - as you can now see. It's the project that I told you about."

Everything was new to Angela. She was crying whilst resting her head on her mother's lap.

"Well, mother and everyone here, I am Angela`s husband." Elijah finally explained who he was.

"What?" Samantha exclaimed.

"Yes, mother," he confirmed.

"It's true, mom," Angela confirmed as well.

Everyone was surprised and speechless. "Mother," Elijah said, "It doesn't matter what you went through: the tears you cried, the embarrassment you felt, the sleepless nights you had. What matters is who you are now."

From today and onwards, consider me as your real son. I will look after you just like my own mother. I have already installed a landline phone in the house for easy communication. Whenever you want anything, feel free to call me at any time. I will always respond immediately.

I have also recruited maids specifically to look after you, and to ensure that this place remains clean all the time. I must confess that I had loved your daughter with all my heart.

For fifteen years in marriage, we have not yet gotten a child. But that has not been bothering me at all, because my love for Angela was unconditional!"

Elijah paused for a minute before continuing. "Before you, mother, Angela, and everyone here, I now declare that it's over between me and Angela. I have already processed divorce papers for you, Angela, to sign. I am sorry. You and I cannot live together anymore!"

Angela was shocked. She knew her husband would be angry, having found out the truth, but did not expect him to ask her for a divorce. When the microphone was handed over to her, she couldn't say much. In tears, she acknowledged her grave mistake. "It's my fault!" she said.

She then walked into the house. As a professional engineer, she appreciated the quality of the work. Having stepped into the sitting room, she looked at the family photo album.

The photos of her father reminded her of the many happy times during her childhood. "I am sorry, dad. Please forgive me!" She wept.

Angela then went into her mother's bedroom. She couldn't stop crying. She remembered all of the promises she had made, but she had not honoured any of them, even though she had the capacity to fulfil them all. She also felt very sorry about deceiving her husband, who had been so attentive and kind; indeed, a model of what a loving husband should be.

She then went back outside and asked for an opportunity to speak once more. Everyone was silent. Some of the residents felt sorry for her while others thought what she had done was unforgivable. Angela said, "all of you who confronted me on my arrival, I don't blame you at all. I can understand the anger you feel towards me. I have done wrong. Please forgive me and accept me back in this village."

Angela confessed that, when she had gone to the University, she had forgotten her family. Like many other students, she made new friends. But in order to fit in with them, she lied about her family background. She acted as if she was from a wealthy family.

She used all of the allowances from her government scholarship to buy expensive items, including clothes, handbags, shoes, earrings and necklaces. Whoever visited her in her hostel room could not doubt her story was true, because of the high quality items she owned.

Angela became one of the proudest students at the University. She even changed her way of walking and speaking. She studied how very wealthy people spoke and then copied their language and accent. Her friends were very accommodating. They didn't care about her.

However, towards the end of their first year at University, one of Angela's friends, Gabriel, suggested that they should visit each other's parents. "Oh, that's true. It's a good idea that our parents get to know us all as friends," Tim agreed.

"So, who should we start with?" he asked.

Hazel suggested that they should start with Angela`s parents.

 "No! No!" Angela exclaimed.

Everyone looked at each other with a puzzled expression. "What is it, Angela? Any problem?" Mike asked.

"I don't understand. We have all agreed that we should visit each other`s parents and now she is opposing it. Why?" Tara demanded.

"Are you not our friend anymore, Angela?" Tabitha inquired.

"It's not like that, guys. We are still friends." Angela said, now looking rather worried.

"Then why?" Tara insisted.

"You see, I never saw my parents. They all passed way when I was only four months old. My grandmother looked after me at her house, but she also passed away recently - during my vacation." Angela said, trying to look and sound confident.

 "Oh, dear! Pardon us, Angela. We didn't know that." Her friends clearly felt sorry for her.

"So you don't even have any relatives? Sara asked her politely.

"Not even one, Sara." Angela replied.

"That's strange! Not even one relative?" Maria doubted her story, but Angela's other friends confronted her.

"It happens. Some people lose their families and relatives in wars or accidents, so maybe it is the same case with her. Isn`t it, Angela?" Michelle asked.

"That's true, Michelle," she replied in a low voice.

"Friends, I think we have to help Angela, now that she doesn't have anyone to stay with. It's up to us to be there for her." Sara suggested.

She then asked Angela if she would like to stay with her at her parents' home during every holiday from the University. Angela accepted without hesitation. At the end of their first year, Sara took Angela and her friends to her parents' home.

Her parents were very happy to meet Angela and their other friends. When Sara told her parents about Angela`s sad story, they felt very sorry for her. They said, "Angela, this is your home. Feel free to come over any time."

"Oh, thank you so much for your kindness." Angela said politely.

From there, Angela did not return home. All of her friends at the University knew her as a double orphan, and they truly felt sorry for her.

Even when Angela met Elijah for the first time, she told him the same story. She also told the same story on their wedding day.

After making her confession, Angela advised the young generation to never make the same mistake she did. "Yes, your parents may not be perfect, but they are the most precious gift God has ever given you." She said.

"So whether your parents are poor, drunkards, uneducated, blind, dumb or lame, never degrade them. Never forget them.

Never deny them before your friends or in public, because parents are irreplaceable! Love them the way they are, and care for them as much as you can," Angela emphasised.

She gave an example of her close friend who had abandoned her father in a nursing home.

Many times her dad cried out wishing to see her, to talk to her but she was always busy with work and her family.

She never cared to visit him until the day he passed on.

When she got the news about his passing, together with her husband they immediately arranged a mega funeral for him.
Such cases unfortunately are very common these days.

We need to change for sure!" Angela concluded.

She then went to Elijah, "I am sorry for everything. Please forgive me. And,"

"And what, Angela?" Elijah interrupted.

He thought she was going to ask him if he would cancel the divorce papers, but she did not. She hugged him and said, "Thank you so much for everything that you have done for my mother and the entire village of Lama. What a big lesson!"

"Thank you too for appreciating, Angela." Elijah replied.

Then Angela decided to stay with her mother for a few days.

However, Elijah went back to the city immediately. When Angela returned to the city, she signed the divorce papers willingly and let Elijah move on.

A few years later, she met and fell in love with Rev. Keith, a Priest from the Anglican Church, whom she introduced to her mother and to the people of Lama.

Later on, the two held their wedding ceremony in the city. Angela had arranged means of transport for her mother and her village mates so they could attend and participate in the function. Samantha felt very happy. In her speech, she wished Angela and her husband the best of luck.

Angela and Rev. Keith now have two beautiful children. And recently, Angela gave her mother a brand new car on the occasion of her 76th birthday party. With her help, Samantha hires a full-time driver.

Angela changed completely! She even remembered Isabella and her husband, who had supported her from the time she joined secondary school up to the time she completed high school.

As an expression of her appreciation for them, Angela built them a well-furnished residential house, as big as her mother's but with a different design.

She vowed that, for as long as she lives, she will take care of her mother, Isabella and her husband.

Angela is also planning to start a University in the area, in memory of her father. Benjamin Memorial University will have excellent lecturers and a wide range of courses and scholarships. Half of the scholarships will be awarded to the less privileged students within Lama Village and in nearby towns.

Amazingly, people in Lama Village have pledged their total support to the project. Isabella and her husband have already offered fifteen acres of land, free of charge, where a memorial University can be built.

Elijah, on the other hand, also remarried. He has a beautiful wife, Dr. Linda. She owns one of the biggest private hospitals in the city. So far, Elijah and Dr. Linda have a son and twin daughters.

Does Elijah still care about Samantha as he pledged?

Yes, he does, and Dr. Linda calls her "mother in –law!" Angela likes Dr. Linda very much. She has now become their family doctor.

Angela respects Elijah a lot for, without him, she would not have returned home and reconciled with her mother and the entire village of Lama. She doesn't look at him as her ex-husband. Rather she looks at him as a mentor and role model.

And according to the people of Lama, from the time Elijah helped in extending electricity in every home in the area, he is looked at as a native son not a stranger.

All in all, Angela is now on the right track, so determined and dedicated to make her childhood dream come true. She hopes that in a few years to come, Lama will be a model village with unique infrastructures in the whole country.

Indeed, a dream never dies! So, just like Angela, you too may have messed up in life in one way or another. But the question is, did you have a dream?

Or do you have a dream? If your answer is yes, then chase it! Stop blaming yourself, stop giving excuses.

Just start now! It's never too late for you to pursue your dreams.

Printed in Great Britain
by Amazon

61822719R00047